MOG
on Fox Night

written and illustrated by
Judith Kerr

HarperCollins *Children's Books*

For Daniel, Rebecca
Katie and Rachelle

More Mog stories to treasure:

Mog the Forgetful Cat Mog on Fox Night
Mog's Christmas Mog and the Granny
Mog and the Baby Mog and the V.E.T.
Mog in the Dark Mog's Bad Thing
Mog's ABC Goodbye Mog
Mog and Bunny

First published in hardback in Great Britain by HarperCollins Publishers Ltd in 1993. First published in paperback by Picture Lions in 1994. This edition published by HarperCollins Children's Books in 2004

28

ISBN: 978-0-00-717136-1

Picture Lions and HarperCollins Children's Books are imprints of HarperCollins Publishers Ltd. HarperCollins Children's Books is a division of HarperCollins Publishers Ltd. Text and illustrations copyright © Kerr-Kneale Productions Ltd 1993. The author/illustrator asserts the moral right to be identified as the author/illustrator of the work. A CIP catalogue record for this title is available from the British Library.

Visit our website at: www.harpercollins.co.uk

Printed in China

One day Mog did not want to eat her supper.
It was fish. But Mog always had an egg for breakfast.
She thought, "Why shouldn't I have an egg for supper as well?"
She looked at the fish. Then she looked at Mrs Thomas.
She made a sad face. "Oh dear," said Mrs Thomas.
"Perhaps that fish isn't very nice."

"I'll give her some kitty food," said Nicky.
Mog looked at the kitty food. Then she looked at Nicky.
She made an even sadder face.

"I know," said Debbie. "She wants an egg."
Just then Mr Thomas came in from the garden.

Mr Thomas had been putting the binbags out
for the binmen to take away in the morning.
Mr Thomas did not like doing the binbags.
He liked it even less when it was snowing,
and he was cross.

He said, "You spoil that cat. That cat has
been given two suppers and has left them both.
She is not to be given an egg as well.
In fact, if that cat does not eat every bit
of those two suppers, she will not get
an egg for her breakfast either."
And he put the egg back in the fridge.

Mog was very sad when the egg went back in the fridge.
She was also very cross. She hissed at Mr Thomas.
Then she hissed at the fridge.

And then
she ran
through her
cat flap
and out into
the garden.

The garden was very cold.
There was snow everywhere.

But there was no snow under the binbags.
Mog crept under a binbag and went to sleep.

Debbie and Nicky were sad too when they went to bed.
"Mog never eats anything she doesn't like," said Debbie.
"She'll never eat that fish and the kitty food."
"And then she won't get an egg for her breakfast,"
said Nicky. "She'll be so cross."

Mog was cross even in her sleep.

She had a cross dream.
It was a dream about Mr Thomas.
Mr Thomas had put all the eggs
in the world into a binbag.
He wanted to take the binbag away.
Mog tried to stop him…

Suddenly she woke up.
There was snow all over her.
The binbag had gone.
Had Mr Thomas taken it away?

She looked.
Then she thought, "This is too much.
First they give me a horrible supper,
and now there's a fox in my garden."
The fox had made a hole in the binbag
and was pulling things out of it.
"What is he doing?" thought Mog.

The fox ate one of the things
he had pulled out of the binbag.
It was a chicken bone.

Then he ate something else.
It was a piece of fish.
Mog knew that piece of fish.
She had left it in her dish the day before.
It had not been nice then.
She thought, "That fox is mad."

Then she saw something else.
The fox had a little fox.
No, he had two little foxes.
He was giving them bits to eat
out of the binbag.

But one of the little foxes
only wanted to play.

It played with the snow.

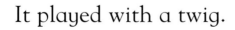

It played with a twig.

It played with an old tin.

And then it wanted to play with Mog.

Mog thought, "I don't want to play with that
little fox," and she ran through her cat flap
and back into the house.

But the little fox ran after her.

And the other little fox ran after the first little fox.

And the big fox ran after them both.

Mog thought, "This is really too much.
First they give me a horrible supper.
Then there's a fox in my garden,
and now there are three foxes in my kitchen."

The foxes liked Mog's kitchen.
They liked the sink.

They liked the pots and pans.

They
liked
the
kitchen
cupboard,

and the breakfast table and Mog's basket.
Mog thought, "There are too many foxes here.
I'm going!"

She found a much nicer
place and went to sleep.

Very early in the morning she woke up.
Debbie woke up too.

Debbie said, "Look who's in my bed.
Why aren't you in your basket, Mog?"
Nicky said, "I wonder if she's eaten her supper."

They went down to the kitchen to see.
Mog's two dishes were empty.
"She's eaten it!" said Nicky.

Then they saw something else.
"I don't think it was Mog who ate it," said Debbie.

The foxes thought it was time to go home.
They ran out through the cat flap.

Then they ran off through the garden.
It had stopped snowing and it was a lovely day.

Debbie and Nicky
tidied the kitchen.

They tidied up every bit.

"Now you can go back in
your basket, Mog," said Nicky.
Just then Mr and Mrs Thomas came in.
Mr Thomas looked at the empty dishes.
"There," he said. "What a good cat.
I knew Mog would eat her supper in the end."

Debbie and Nicky said nothing.
After all, they thought, no one really
knew *who* had eaten Mog's supper.

Mog had

a lovely egg

for her breakfast.

She was very pleased.

And the foxes were pleased too.